George Huddesford

Salmagundi

A Miscellaneous Combination of Original Poetry

George Huddesford

Salmagundi
A Miscellaneous Combination of Original Poetry

ISBN/EAN: 9783744780407

Printed in Europe, USA, Canada, Australia, Japan

Cover: Foto ©Andreas Hilbeck / pixelio.de

More available books at **www.hansebooks.com**

ORIGINAL POETRY.

Wanton ye Graces round his banquet tower.

CONTENTS.

CONTENTS.

SALMAGUNDI;

A MISCELLANEOUS COMBINATION OF

ORIGINAL POETRY:

CONSISTING OF

ILLUSIONS OF FANCY;

AMATORY, ELEGIAC, LYRICAL, EPIGRAMMATICAL,

AND OTHER

PALATABLE INGREDIENTS.

- - - - - - - - - - - - - - - SOLUM
POSCIMUS UT CŒNES CIVILITER.
JUVENAL, SAT. V.

LONDON:

PRINTED BY T. BENSLEY, BOLT COURT, FLEET STREET;

FOR T. PAYNE, MEWS GATE; B. WHITE AND SON, FLEET STREET;
AND J. DEBRET, PICCADILLY.

1791.

TO

RICHARD WYATT, ESQ.

OF MILTON PLACE, SURRY:

IN ACKNOWLEDGMENT OF THE EDITOR'S OBLIGATIONS

TO HIS

LIBERAL AND LONG EXPERIENCED FRIENDSHIP,

THIS PUBLICATION IS DEDICATED,

WITH

RESPECT AND GRATITUDE.

ILLUSIONS OF FANCY.

TO RICHARD WYATT, ESQ.

ON LEAVING HIS MANSION, AFTER ASCOT RACES.

———— ME LUDIT AMABILIS

INSANIA.   HOR. LIB. 3. CARM. 4.

ILLUSIONS OF FANCY.

CONGENIAL to my penfive breaft,
O'erfhadowing clouds the fkies inveft;
Faft-falling fhowers deform the glade,
No cheering ray difpels the fhade,
No lark's clear carol wakes the morn
That low'ring bids my fteps forlorn
Abandon SURRY's fmiling plains,
Fly the Lov'd Roof where Friendfhip reigns,
Circling whofe hofpitable hearth
Fair Freedom, Senfe, and liberal Mirth,
Their heart-enlivening influence fhed;
Where Time throws off his wings of lead,
And, clad in purple plumage light,
Speeds fwifter than the winds his flight.

Thence, as my devious courfe I fteer,
FANCY, in fairy vifions clear,
Bids, to beguile my 'tranced eyes,
Paft joys in fweet fucceffion rife:
Refrefhing airs fhe bids me breathe
Where, ASCOT, thine enchanting Heath,
Impregnated with mild perfume,
Bares its broad bofom's purple bloom:
Gives me to view the fplendid croud,
The high-born racer neighing loud,
The manag'd fteeds that fide by fide
Precede the glittering chariot's pride,
Within whofe filken coverture
Some peerlefs Beauty fits fecure,
And, fatal to the foul's repofe,
Around her thrilling glances throws.

Hence, FANCY, wing thy rapid flight
O'er oaks in deepeft verdure dight,

Whofe writhed limbs of giant mould
Wave to the breeze their umbrage bold;
Bear me, embowering fhades between,
Through many a glade and vifta green,
Whence filver ftreams are feen to glide,
And towering domes th' horizon hide,
To LEONARD's foreft-fringed Mound; ᵃ
Where lavifh Nature fpreads around
Whate'er can captivate the fight,
Elyfian lawns, and profpects bright,
As vifions of expiring faints,
Or fcenes that HARCOURT's pencil paints.
Bear me where, 'midft enamell'd meads,
Redundant Thames his bounty fheds,
Teeming with many a plenteous freight:
Where o'er the vale, in antique ftate
Imperial WINDSOR's turrets frown,
And maffy fanes of old renown.
Give me to gaze with ardent eye
On gorgeous fpoils of Chivalry;

To ken aloft the radiant rows
Of banners won from Britain's foes:
Recall the glorious deeds of yore;
Shew the dark mail that EDWARD wore;
The falchion shew, whofe thund'ring ftroke
Creffy's pale ranks impetuous broke;
From whofe fell glare appall'd with dread
Proud Gallia's trembling chieftains fled,
Or on its edge deftruction found,
And dyed with regal gore the ground.

Give me, fair FANCY, to pervade
Chambers in pictur'd pomp array'd!
Peopling whofe ftately walls I view
The godlike forms that RAFFAELLE drew;
I feem to fee his magic hand
Wield the wondrous pencil-wand,
Whofe touches animation give,
And bid th' infenfate canvafs live;

Glowing with many a deed divine
Achiev'd in holy Paleftine.
The Paffions feel its potent charm,
And round the mighty mafter fwarm;
Lo, where Dismay with haggard gaze [b]
The death-fmote Hypocrite furveys;
Beholds his eyes convulfive roll,
And Fate arreft his fordid foul!---

Lo! motionlefs Attention ftands, [c]
Where to the firmament his hands
Sublime the great Inftructor rears!
While Athens, rapt in wonder, hears
Truth's energetic voice proclaim
Her unknown God's tremendous name!---

Deep read in fuperftition's lore,
Behold capricious Zeal adore [d]

(In sublunary weeds array'd)

The fabled Gods her fears have made!

" Those pow'rful sounds," she cries, " I know:

" Hark! from the honied lips they flow

" Of MAIA's Son!---Can Man difpenfe

" Activity to impotence?

" Can energy of mortal hand

" The shrunk, distorted limb expand?

" Inveterate force of ills confound,

" And bid the lame with tranfport bound?---

" 'Tis Jove's,---the unexampled deed!

" To Jove th' Ifaurian Steer shall bleed!

" To Jove the rich libations pour!

" Braid in bright wreaths each blooming flow'r,

" Swell each loud strain of festive mirth,

" To gratulate the Gods on earth!"---

Artift supreme! by nature taught

To clothe with life each glowing thought,

Too foon the Deftinies confpire
To quench thy pencil's glorious fire;
Too foon the foul that warm'd thy clay
Afpir'd to realms of endlefs day,
On wings of ecftafy, to join
Sages and faints, a band divine,
Whofe awful forms (ere death withdrew
The veil that darkens mortal view)
Heav'n bade thy penetrative eye
Amid her dazzling courts defcry;
Thence bade thee trace the faultlefs line,
Th' expreffive grace, the chafte defign,
The mien that love and awe infpires,
And wakes Devotion's pureft fires.
Thy memory, ftill to genius dear,
Britain's enlighten'd fons revere;
And grateful hail their Monarch's name,
Whofe liberal care thy labours claim:
To heights impervious heretofore
Who bids immortal fcience foar;

c

Far feen in venerable pride,
Whofe regal feat, expanding wide
Its portals at his high beheft,
Hails ev'ry Art an honour'd gueft:
Beneath whofe mild aufpicious reign
The Genius old of Greece again,
Awaken'd from his deep repofe,
In REYNOLDS' living canvafs glows;
(Where Grace and Energy divine
With Beauty truly blent combine)
And braids his deathlefs bays around
The BRITISH RAFFAELLE's brows renown'd.
Lo! by his daring hand pourtray'd,e
The fanguinary fcene difplay'd
Where martial peers, in glittering mail,
Unfold their pennons to the gale;
O'er Normandy's difmantled plains
Where iron-clad CONTENTION reigns;
And HAVOC waits (his treffes wet
With gore) thy nod, PLANTAGENET!

Wafted from Albion's Ifle afar,
Where wake her fons the ftorm of war;
Where, ravifh'd from the parent ftem
To grace the Victor's diadem,
Thy Lilies, France, no more affume
The fplendour of their wonted bloom;
No more with peerlefs luftre glow,
But foil with blood their native fnow!---

Now o'er the braid from FANCY's loom
The rich tints breathe a deeper gloom;
While, confecrated domes beneath,
Midft hoary fhrines and caves of death,
Secluded from the eye of day,
She bids her penfive votary ftray:
Brooding o'er monumental cells,
Where awe-diffufing SILENCE dwells;
Save when along the lofty fane
DEVOTION wakes her hallow'd ftrain,

When the vaſt Organ's breathing frame
Echoes the voice of loud acclaim,
And the deep diapaſon's ſound
Thunders the vaulted iles around.
From the broad window's fretted height
Streams the rich flood of mellow'd light,
That bids the pav'd expanſe below
With hues of gold and crimſon glow,
Reflected from the gorgeous pane,
Where PICTURE holds her laſting reign :
Where, in tranſlucent glories dight,
Celeſtial forms arreſt the ſight ;
Th' enraptur'd gazer's pow'rs control,
And bathe in ecſtaſy the ſoul.
While rang'd in reverend majeſty,
The taper ſhafts aſcending high,
To decorate the criſped roof,
Their mingling branches ſhoot aloof ;
Where, blazon'd in projecting gold,
Flame the proud creſts of Barons bold.

Now beams on FANCY's eye no more
The ſpangled roof, the poliſh'd floor,
The ſpeaking chryſtal's various ſtain,
Illumining the wondrous fane:
Choirs, altars, ſhrines, illuſive fade.---
Enliv'ning Airs my ſenſe invade;
Encircled by the young and fair,
The blithe ASSEMBLY's bliſs I ſhare;
Swift o'er the lyre's harmonious ſtrings
His magic hand the minſtrel flings;
Obedient to the ſprightly found,
The dancer's quivering feet rebound;
Diffuſing wide their ſilver rays,
Aloft the ſparkling luſtres blaze;
While milder emanations flow
From love-enkindling orbs below.
Here, peerleſs CHESHIRE, I behold
Thy looſe robe float in airy fold!

Tall as the pine's cerulean creft,

Encircling plumes thy brows inveft,

Amid whofe fnowy fummits high

Infidious Cupids ambufh'd lie.

To each enchanting Grace allied,

Here FANCY bids fair BOUVERIE glide,

Light as the breath of opening morn

O'er beds of unfunn'd violets borne;

And every captive heart furprife,

Unconfcious of her victories.

There TOWNSHEND threads the pleafing maze:

Ah who can unenamour'd gaze!

How fhall my bofom freedom know

Where LAW's ingenuous beauties glow!

Frefh as the fpring, as Hebe fair,

Where Egham fends a gentle Pair,

And bids the charm'd affections hail

The SISTER LILIES of her Vale;

Whofe bloom difdains fictitious aid,

Lovelieft amid feclufion's fhade.---

The meafures ceafe---her tempting ftores
Around prolific FANCY pours;
The fumptuous board, extended wide,
Her vifionary viands hide:
Beauty and youth the banquet fhare---
Hence to the winds intrufive Care!
Fly, haggard Spleen, the glad abode
Where holds his ftate the Rofy God!
Where Cytherea, hand in hand,
The Graces leads, a blifsful band;
Where Comus to his feftive rites,
To joy and genial cheer, invites;
Where Frolic, Sport, and Jollity,
Await their queen, Euphrofyne;
And Love, around her hovering,
Beats the light air with fapphire wing;
With luftre fhed from Beauty's eyes
Gilds his gay veft of thoufand dyes,
Whofe undulating folds difpenfe
Caffia's ambrofial redolence.

Crown'd with each lovely charmer's name,
I fee the ruddy nectar flame!
Latent amid th' infpiring draught
Speeds the blind God his fubtle fhaft;
And, while the flafk his votary drains,
Defpotic in his bofom reigns;
Whence, for the Nymph his foul admires,
Th' involuntary figh expires,
And languor fteals through every vein.---
Now to the fprightly dance again!
Wing'd with delight and melody,
Swift let the jocund moments fly,
Startling the fombrous reign of Night;
'Till, heav'n's blue arch afcending bright,
Aurora the wide welkin ftreaks
With rofes, fuch as Chloe's cheeks
Amid encircling fnows reveal,
When her foft palms love's preffure feel.
Till Sol his fteeds of golden hoof
Drives through revolving fpheres aloof;

And wakes the blooms that odours breathe,
Enliv'ning earth and air beneath;
And o'er old Ocean's boundlefs deeps
His regal robe of glory fweeps.
Then home they hie, and, warm with wine,
Still, as they prefs the couch fupine,
See fairy-vifions round them float,
Lift the foft lyre's imperfect note,
Exhauft th' imaginary vafe,
Fair forms in faultering meafures chafe,
Catch from bright eyes the melting beam,
And of Ideal Tranfports dream.

O Fancy! bleft Enchantrefs, deign
Still to prolong thy blifsful reign!
Frequent to footh my languid fenfe,
Thy vifionary balm difpenfe!
Inveft in varying colours bright
Each grateful fcene of paft delight!

Sweet dalliance let me hold with THEE,
Eftrang'd from SAD REALITY!

O deign to cheer my humble cell!
Thence grave Parochial Cares expel:
Shield me from Swathed Infants' fcream,
And clouds of fuffocating fteam
That from the Goffip's bowl exhale,
Mix'd with Tobacco's potent gale!
From Undertakers' gloomy brows,
From Overfeers' important bows,
From ruthlefs Sexton's lethal face,
And Beadles briftled o'er with lace!
Shield me from puritanic cant
Of faded Maids, who matins haunt; f
And, lowering o'er each lonely pew,
At once their fins and wrinkles rue!
My trembling ears, O FANCY, fave
From Sternhold's inharmonious ftave!

From the fad Brief's unpitied tale,
From Expofition trite and ftale,
And many an opiate Inference!
Shield me from founds at ftrife with fenfe!
From Pedantry of formal port,
And Confequence in Caffoc fhort!---

So, Goddefs, thy propitious fmile,
Shall Time's ungenial flight beguile;
Wake into joy my torpid hours,
And ftrew life's barren path with flow'rs.
Nor fhall the kindred Mufe decline
To blend her fimple blooms with thine ;
Bleft, if the wreath by FANCY wove
Kind Friendfhip's partial voice approve ;
Nor figh for unfubftantial bays
If WYATT's plaudit crown her lays.

AMATORY ODES.

O D E I.

Lᴇᴛ the fons of Lᴜᴄʀᴇ pine
For glittering heaps of golden ore,
To fwell th' accumulated ftore
Contemn the terrors of the mine;
Explore the caverns dark and drear
Mantled around with deadly dew;
Where congregated vapours blue,
Fir'd by the taper glimmering near,
Bid dire explofion the deep realms invade,
And earth-born light'nings gleam athwart th' infernal fhade.

Pʀɪᴅᴇ, on thy vefture's purple fold
Let the fky-tinctured fapphire blaze,
. The emerald fhed its milder rays,
And rubies blufh in circling gold: .

Low at thy nod let fuppliants bow,
And crefted chiefs precedence yield;
Thy hand the rod of empire wield,
And wreaths of triumph grace thy brow.---
A nobler aim let my ambition own,
Be LOVE my empire, LESBIA's heart my throne!

Where into rage the wintry blaft
Awakes old Ocean's briny wave
Let COMMERCE urge her bufy flave;
And elevate his trembling maft
Above the billowy precipice,
To meet the forked light'ning's flafh;
Then down th' advent'rous veffel dafh,
Found'ring within the black abyfs:
Or let his freight fecure the furges fweep,
And of their prey defraud the monfters of the deep:

My bark the tide of young defire,
O Venus, to thy happy realm
Shall waft, fair Hope direct the helm,
Love's fighs the fwelling fails infpire:
To Thee, bright Offspring of the wave,
I'll many an amorous vow prefer:
From ftorms of hate thy mariner
And blaft of chill indiff'rence fave!
So to thy pow'r I'll frame the votive lay,
And moor'd in LESBIA's arms confefs thy fov'reign fway.

Amid enfanguin'd fields of War,
VALOUR, be thy Votary found;
Where crimfon banners wave around
The martial clarion, echoing far;
In vain gigantic Terror calls
His fpectre fhapes, a ghaftly band: ---
Nor Difcord, hurling high his brand,
Nor Danger's horrid front appals;

E

Nor Death his fierce unconquer'd foul can tame,
Or from his grafp withhold the glorious meed of Fame.

But let me wander far away
From the loud drum and neighing fteed,
Thro' many a panfie-painted mead,
Where Ifis' bright-hair'd Naiads ftray;
High o'er my head a pendant bow'r
Let the broad elm and branching pine
With intermingling umbrage twine;
There Love's impaffion'd fong I'll pour,
And fummon every wave that dances near,
Bridling his wanton fpeed, my LESBIA's praife to hear.

Where the pale lamp's waining eye
At eve, from out the cloyfter'd nook
Cafts o'er the gloom a lingering look,
There let THE SAGE his labours ply;

And many a feat of Champion bold,

And many a legendary rhime

Snatch from the Sepulchre of Time;

And frequent, as the night grows old,

At fear-engender'd forms recoil aghaſt,

And hear unhallow'd ghoſts wail in each hollow blaſt.

But o'er my haunts with influence bland

Let ev'ning fling her welcome ſhade:

Then mid the dance, O beauteous maid!

Let me thine un-reluctant hand

Enraptur'd ſeize:---or let the Lyre,

Obedient to thy ſoft control,

Bind in harmonious chains my ſoul,

And ecſtaſy and bliſs inſpire;

While to the charmed ear in heav'nly ſtrains,

Enamour'd of thy touch, each trembling chord complains.

Then, Faireft, let my bofom feel
Thy fmile's exhilarating pow'r,
Grateful as, mid noon's fultry hour,
The Grot where trickling dews congeal:
And, in the rich grape's purple tide
When Joy and genial Pleafure fwim,
Do Thou but kifs its chryftal brim,
And, to thy bard the goblet guide;
So fhall my fong exalt thy praife above
Hebe, who bids o'erflow the nectar'd cup of Jove.

ODE II.

———————

Now hath the Sun his evanescent fires
Quench'd in the billows of the western main;
Cease their soft carols all the feather'd choirs,
And gloomy solitude usurps the plain.

Rise, ye deep shades, ye waves in darkness roll,
Ye feather'd choirs to silence yield the grove,
For LESBIA sleeps:---nor cheers my pensive soul
The glance of rapture, nor the voice of love.

Ye Winds, whose havoc-spreading pinions ply
Their furious speed, and with dire yell invade
This nether world, whose wasteful tyranny
Pale Dryads mourn in many a ruin'd shade;

Wake not my Love:---Let not your thund'ring cry
With dread alarm the haunt of peace infeft;
Here breathe in foft Æolian melody
Each cadence fweet that charms the foul to reft.

Ye Spectres (whom belated pilgrims fear,
Iffuing in throngs from charnel, vault, or tomb,
What time deep-fhadowing clouds thy radiant fphere,
Cynthia, involve in night's meridian gloom,)

Hence to deferted fane or mouldering hall,
Or the gaunt felon's ruthlefs courfe control;
With monitory fhrick the wretch appal,
And to compunction wake his torpid foul.

But walk not near the couch where LESBIA lies
Like fome rich pearl in its enamell'd fhell,
Or fainted relic, from profaner eyes
Secluded in the dim fhrine's filver cell.

Wanton, ye Fairies, round her tranquil bow'r,
With blifsful elves fantaftic meafures tread;
O'er her foft eyelids dews of opiate pow'r,
Cull'd from choice blooms, in fhow'rs of fragrance fhed:

Let your bright tapers' vifionary ray
The raven-tinctur'd robe of Night illume;
And, ftreaming o'er your fpangled crefts, difplay
The wave-enamour'd halcyon's emerald plume.

And bid your Minftrel-Fays, a fhadowy choir,
That charm the planets from their fpheres fublime,

Celeftial fongs, that love and joy infpire,
Chant to their golden harp's harmonious chime.

And, when morn's purple ftreaks th' horizon ftain,
And Fairies fly the peal of Chanticleer,
Let Fancy ftill your glittering hues retain,
Still let your wild notes tremble on her ear.---

Then, LESBIA, wake thy beauties, frefher far
Than Galatea boafted when fhe lav'd
In the fmooth Deep her coral-axled car,
And the ftern heart of Neptune's fon enflav'd.

Wake at His Call, to footh whofe foul in vain
Morn fheds her radiant beam, her od'rous airs,
Save when, attentive to his artlefs ftrain,
That radiant beam, thofe odours LESBIA fhares.

He afks no laureate wreath to deck his brows,

No golden meed his bounded wifhes claim,

Bleft if the Object of his tendereft vows

Smile on his lay---for LESBIA's fmile is Fame.

ODE III.

Fate gave with unrelenting fpeed to fly
The genial hours that Love and LESBIA blefs'd;
Sad, on her ear I pour'd the parting figh,
Sad, on her hand the parting kifs imprefs'd.

Nor LESBIA, generous maid, her hand withdrew,
Nor did her ear difdain the parting figh;
Swift to her cheek the living crimfon flew,
Soft pity fill'd her breaft and fympathy.

There all the gentle Charities refide
With liberal Sentiment and chafte Defire,
And banifh cold Referve and ruthlefs Pride,
That bid Affection's trembling flame expire.

" Farewell the Bard,"---she cried---" whose grateful Muse
" Bade many a vocal shade my name resound:
" And, rich in Fancy's visionary hues,
" With many a fairy wreath my tresses bound:

" Still on those artless wreaths shall LESBIA smile,
" Still shall her partial voice applaud thy lay,
" Bid unexpected joy thy cares beguile,
" And Hope's pure radiance gild each rising day."---

Ah! far from Love, from LESBIA, doom'd to fly,
Cheerless and sad 1 trace life's gloomy scene,
And faintly Hope's far distant ray descry,
While clouds and darkness fill the void between!

The feaman thus the Beacon's friendly fires
Dejected views, while the black billows fwell,
And from the haven that his foul defires
Remorfelefs winds his labouring bark repel.

What lenitive can eafe the bofom's pain,
What charm the fever of the mind remove?
Can Solitude, can Silence, break the chain
That's forg'd by friendfhip, fympathy, and love?

Then let me fhun the Day-ftar's glittering beam
And feek in folitary glens repofe:
O'er the rufh'd margin of fome lingering ftream,
Where the broad oak his grateful umbrage throws.

Or thro' fome Cloyfter's dim receffes rove,
O'er hollow founding vaults and cells of death;

To all the foft anxieties of love
Infenfible as thofe that fleep beneath.

Delufive hope!---Say, where the folitude
That to intrufive Love accefs denies?
Say, where the hallow'd haunt whofe glooms exclude
LESBIA's enchanting form from Fancy's eyes?---

Then bid the flood that fwells the wanton vine
O'erflow the lucid vafe with rofes crown'd;
Prepare the feaft---and let the God of wine
Bathe with his purple balm my amorous wound!

Let the ripe clufter's animating tide
Pervade with genial flow my languid frame,
Till Paffion's fad folicitudes fubfide,
Till fades, all pow'rful Love, thy fatal flame.

Ah! midft the Sons of Revelry in vain
Thy captive, LESBIA, ftruggles to be free!
God of the grape, thy goblets while I drain,
Still fways my breaft Love's mightier Deity!---

Let Harmony from her enchanting fhell
Pour the fweet Note that fooths affliction's figh:
Now the full chord's deep modulation fwell,
Now wake the joy-infpiring fymphony;

Such as refounding from thy golden ftrings,
Divine Alcæus, charm'd Hell's fhadowy throng;
While combatants renown'd and vanquifh'd kings
Fir'd the bold ftrains of thine immortal fong. s

Say, could the voice of melody fubdue
The pangs that tortur'd Ghofts were doom'd to bear,
And lull to ftrange repofe the Serpent-crew
That hifs, Alecto, in thine iron hair?

Then let the cares that rend a Lover's breaft
The magic of that voice refiftlefs prove.---
Still breathes th' enamour'd Bard his fond requeft
In vain---for Mufic is the food of Love.

In each wild fong that wakes the vale around
My Fair-one's fafcinating voice I hear;
And Fancy bids the foft lute's filver found
Waft her mild accents to my ravifh'd ear.

Sweet the wild fong that wakes the valley,---Sweet
Warbles the foft lute's melancholy note:

But founds with richer melody replete
From LESBIA's lips on gales of fragrance float.---

Not Mufic, Wine, nor Solitude, can quell
The tumults that this bleeding bofom knows.
Then vifit, God of Sleep, my penfive cell,
And to my foul reftore its loft repofe!

Aufpicious to my pray'r the gloomy God
Bids the deep fhadows of the Night arife;
O'er my lone couch extends his fable rod,
And feals with opiate charm his fuppliant's eyes.

Ah! whence That Virgin Bloom, on night's dun pall
Whofe glance with pity's mild effulgence beams?
Fair Sov'reign of my foul, at Fancy's call,
'Tis LESBIA comes to blefs her Poet's dreams!

G

(Dazzling the Phrygian Boy's enraptur'd fight
Not Venus 'felf with charms that rivall'd thine,
'Mid the broad fhades of Ida's piny height
To beauty's meed preferr'd her claim divine!)

She beckons me thro' Fairy glades to ftray,
O'er fands of gold where liquid chryftal roves ;
Where drinks unclouded Summer's genial ray
Incenfe exhal'd from aromatic Groves :

Where, o'er each fhadowy dell and oak-crown'd fteep,
Celeftial forms in bright fucceffion glide ;
Where light-train'd Nymphs th' unbending bloffoms fweep,
Or rife in radiance from the tranquil tide :

Where, Lesbia, as I raife the fong to Thee,
The lift'ning Fauns their antic dance refrain,
And dulcet founds of airy minftrelfy
From harps unfeen accompany the ftrain.

And while th' impaffion'd lay thy praifes breathes
Each ruder gale fubfides, th' expanding flow'rs
More lavifh fweets difpenfe, and living wreaths
Of brighter green array the magic bow'rs.

And Love, light hovering in the balmy air,
Fires his proud torch and nerves his golden bow,
And braids his rofeate bands for Thee, my Fair,
And bids thy breaft his gentleft tranfports know.

Thine eyes confefs his pow'r:---Stay waining Night!
Start not, Hyperion, from thine orient goal!

Ye blisful dreams, ye visions of delight,
Ye dear delusions, still possess my soul!

Dissolving at th' unwelcome gleam of dawn,
The Spell that sway'd my captive sense expires.---
No liquid chrystal laves the fairy lawn;
No viewless Minstrels wake celestial lyres;

No spicy groves unfading foliage spread;
Beneath their nectarine freight no branches bend;
No Sylvan bands fantastic measures tread;
No pearl-crown'd Sisters from the wave ascend.

The laughing meads where flow'rs spontaneous grew,
The landscape's various grace, the genial skies,
In cloudless azure drefs'd, elude my view;
And glowing Fancy's fair creation dies.

But thou, bleft Object of my hopes and fears,
Still fhall the Mufe's living meed be thine,
While Grace enchants, while Gentlenefs endears,
While admiration bends at Beauty's fhrine:

Deep grav'n by Love thine image ne'er fhall fade
While Memory in my breaft maintains her feat;
And when for Thee it beats not, Lovely Maid!
Each trembling pulfe of life fhall ceafe to beat.

O D E IV.

TO LESBIA'S LUTE.

Y<small>E</small> trembling ſtrings, from whoſe vibration flows
Joy's thrilling tide and ſadly pleaſing woe:
Soothing the ſenſe, yet to the ſoul's repoſe
Deſtructive as the Nerve of Cupid's Bow!

With gentleſt melody in L<small>ESBIA</small>'s ear
(If any mortal ſounds have pow'r to tell)
Whiſper how much I hope---how much I fear---
The pity I implore---the pains I feel.

When her fleet touch calls forth th' enlivening ſtrain
Bid rapture float upon the charmed air:
Tell her, when ſad th' expreſſive notes complain:
" So breathes thy bard the ſigh of deep deſpair."

Of yore fuch founds, as thrill th' enamour'd breaft
When LESBIA's hands the filver chords embrace,
Could lull th' embattled elements to reft,
Bend knotted oaks, and tame a ruthlefs race;

Yet, LESBIA! like thy lute tho' Orpheus ftrung
His lyre to ftrains divine, its amorous lord
For Thee had left Euridice unfung,
And Pluto's gloomy confines unexplor'd.

O D E V.

NAIAD, unseen of mortal eyes,
Whose light steps haunt this current lone,
Where gentle Zephyr's balmy sighs,
With thy wild wave in unison,
Blend their aërial melodies;

Let me to thy deserted shades
Reveal the never-dying flame
That all my pensive soul pervades,
And teach thine echoes LESBIA's name
E'er the soft light of evening fades!

Unheard, unnotic'd, let me rove
Thy trembling osier wreaths among,

H

And woo the Mufe where none reprove
Affection's unambitious fong,
Nor chide the plaint of hopelefs love.

There, when the Day's dim eyelids clofe,
Hide me within fome fhadowy cave;
And, minift'ring to calm repofe,
Oh foftly bid thy babbling wave
Kifs the dank fedge that round it grows!

No Angler's cruel arts are mine,
Ye timid Tenants of the brook!
Wrought by my hand no viewlefs line,
Difguis'd by me no treacherous hook,
Bids you your little lives refign.

Nor this pellucid rill refrain
To fip, Ye Minftrels of the air!
Your downy plumage to diftain
With blood no fatal Tube I bear,
Nor pay with death your artlefs ftrain.

That Breaft no favage fports can fhare,
Where glow Affection's generous fires:
Soft Pity finds her manfion there,
All whom the breath of life infpires
By her own forrows taught to fpare.

Mine, Gentle NAIAD, be the dell
Whofe clear ftream laves thy chryftal grot:
Near its green margin let me dwell,
By all but One dear Maid forgot,
And bid a world of cares farewell.

Oft let me view thy trembling tide
Chequer'd with Cynthia's filver light,
What time, in Fancy's train defcried,
Before my fafcinated fight
Paft Joy's illufive phantoms glide.

Hopelefs of happier hours to come,
No more array'd in flattering hues
For me the buds of Pleafure bloom:
Yet deigns, at Fancy's call, the Mufe
To gild Affliction's deepening gloom.

With Lesbia's praife the ftrain fhall glow;
Oh may fhe tafte each blifs fupreme
That Hope can paint, or Love beftow;
And calm as Glym's fequefter'd ftream
May her life's gentle current flow!

Wind, Lovely Brook, thy murmuring way,
Still with my forrows fympathize:
So may thy banks frefh flow'rs inlay,
Thy waves in rich redundance rife,
Mild Zephyrs on thy bofom play!

If Zephyr fhould his breath deny,
My fighs fhall fan thy flowery beds;
If parching winds thy channel dry,
The tears defponding Paffion fheds
Shall its exhaufted ftream fupply.

E L E G Y.

WRITTEN AT SEA.

ON Sapphire throne, o'er Heav'n's unnumber'd fires,
The Moon in full-orb'd majefty prefides;
Calm are the feas, a favouring breeze tranfpires,
And thro' the waves the veffel fmoothly glides:

Beyond th' horizon's bound the mind extends,
To the fought fhores where Hope delufive leads:
Sooth'd by the fcene her tortures grief fufpends,
For abfent kindred, friends, and native meads.

Till Sympathy from brooding Memory's ftores
Culls thorns, and plants them in the bleeding breaft;
Sunk into gloom the mind no more explores
Hope's future dawn, and pants in vain for reft.

What tho' the feas are calm, the fkies ferene,
Thus anguifh dictates the defponding ftrain:
" To friendfhip fear prefents a gloomier fcene,
" The whirlwind's fury and tempeftuous main.

" Even now perhaps from many a kindred eye
" My dubious fate compels the trickling tear,
" And ev'ry paffing cloud that veils the fky
" Chills fome fond anxious breaft with boding fear.

" In my Love's bofom deeper forrows roll,
" Frantic with dread fhe fighs, implores, fhe raves;
" Whilft Horror paints me, to her fickening foul,
" Dafh'd on a rock, or whelm'd beneath the waves."

FATHER OF HEAV'N, whofe power controls the ftorms,
O let thy mercy hear a wanderer's pray'r!
Check the wild fears connubial fondnefs forms,
And fave the tender Mourner from defpair.

For Me, whate'er thy fov'reign will fhall doom,
Still give me faith to bear that lot refign'd:
That Faith which, fmiling, courts the dreary tomb,
And, Heav'n-afpiring, fooths th' afflicted mind.

PHILEMON,

AN ELEGY.

WHERE shade yon yews the Churchyard's lonely bourn,
With faultering step, abforb'd in thought profound,
PHILEMON wends in folitude to mourn,
While Evening pours her deep'ning glooms around.

Loud fhrieks the blaft, the fleety torrent drives,
Wide fpreads the tempeft's defolating power;
To grief alone PHILEMON recklefs lives,
No rolling peal he heeds, cold blaft or fhower.

For This the Date that ftampt his EMMA's doom,
In his fond arms fhe breath'd her life's laft figh:
" Say, will my Love e'er feek his EMMA's tomb?"
She cried, then clos'd in death each wiftful eye.

No fighs he breath'd, for anguifh riv'd his breaft,
Her clay-cold hand he grafp'd, no tears he fhed,
'Till fainting Nature funk by grief opprefs'd,
And ere Diftraction came, all fenfe was fled.

Now Time has calm'd, not cur'd PHILEMON's woe,
For grief like his, life-woven never dies;
And ftill each year's collected forrows flow,
As drooping o'er his EMMA's tomb he fighs.

LATIN IMITATION OF STANZAS,

EXTRACTED FROM GAY'S FABLE OF

THE POET AND THE ROSE.

ORIGINAL.

Go Rose, my Chloe's bosom grace!
How happy should I prove,
Might I supply that envied place
With never fading love!
There, Phœnix like, beneath her eye,
Involv'd in fragrance, burn and die!

Know, hapless Flow'r, that thou shalt find
More fragrant roses there:
I see thy with'ring head reclin'd
With envy and despair!
One common fate we both must prove;
You die with Envy, I with Love.

IDEM LATINÈ REDDITUM.

I, ROSA, deliciæ florum, properare memento
Quà niveo invitat pectore pulchra CHLOE!
O, mihi si liceat tali requiescere nido,
Quàm vellem vestro nuncius ire loco!
Sic, O sic positum, rari Phœnicis ad instar,
Fragranti extinctum morte perire juvat!

At, Flos infelix, caveas! formosius ardet,
Dulcè magis redolet, candidus iste sinus:
Vincendi Nympham spem frustrà pascis inanem;
En folia arescunt, ecce recline caput!
Et Flos et Dominus fato moriuntur eodem,
Te Flamma Invidiæ, Me meus urit Amor.

WHITSUNTIDE.

WRITTEN AT WINCHESTER COLLEGE ON THE IMMEDIATE
APPROACH OF THE HOLIDAYS.

HENCE, Thou Fur-clad Winter, fly;
Sire of shivering poverty!
Who, as thou creep'st with chilblains lame
To the crowded charcoal flame,
With chattering teeth and ague cold,
Scarce thy shaking sides canst hold
Whilst Thou draw'st the deep cough out :
God of Foot-ball's noisy rout,
Tumult loud and boist'rous play,
The dangerous slide, the snow-ball fray.

But come, Thou genial Son of Spring,
WHITSUNTIDE, and with thee bring

K

Cricket, nimble boy and light,
In flippers red and drawers white,
Who o'er the nicely-meafur'd land
Ranges around his comely band,
Alert to intercept each blow,
Each motion of the wary Foe.

Or patient take thy quiet ftand,
The Angle trembling in thy hand,
And mark, with penetrative eye,
Kiffing the wave, the frequent fly;
Where the trout with eager fpring
Forms the many-circled ring,
And, leaping from the filver tide,
Turns to the fun his fpeckled fide.

Or lead where Health, a Naiad fair
With rofy check and dropping hair,

From the fultry noon-tide beam,
Dives in ITCHIN's cryftal ftream.
Thy Votaries, rang'd in order due,
TOMORROW's wifh'd-for Dawn fhall view
Greeting the radiant Star of Light
With Matin Hymn and early Rite:
E'en now, thefe hallow'd haunts among,
To Thee we raife the Choral Song; h
And fwell with echoing minftrelfy
The ftrain of joy and liberty.

If pleafures fuch as thefe await
Thy genial reign, with heart elate
For Thee I throw my gown afide,
And hail thy coming, WHITSUNTIDE.

CHRISTMAS.

HENCE, Summer, indolently laid
To fleep beneath the cooling fhade!
Panting quick with fultry heat,
Thirft and faint Fatigue retreat!

Come, CHRISTMAS, father Thou of mirth,
Patron of the feftive hearth,
Around whofe focial ev'ning flame
The jovial fong, the winter game,
The chafe renew'd in merry tale,
The feafon's carols never fail.
Who, tho' the Winter chill the fkies,
Canft catch the glow of exercife,
Following fwift the foot-ball's courfe;
Or with unrefifted force,

Where Frost arrefts the harden'd tide,
Shooting 'crofs the rapid flide.
Who, e'er the mifty morn is grey,
To fome high covert hark'ft away;
While Sport, on lofty courfer borne,
In concert winds his echoing horn
With the deeply-thund'ring hounds,
Whofe clangour wild, and joyful founds,
While Echo fwells the doubling cry,
Shake the woods with harmony.
How does my eager bofom glow
To give the well-known TALLY-HO!
Or fhew, with cap inverted, where
Stole away the cautious hare.
Or, if the blaft of Winter keen
Spangles o'er the filvery green,
Booted high thou lov'ft to tread
Marking, thro' the fedgy mead,
Where the creeping moor-hen lies,
Or fnipes with fudden twitt'ring rife.

Or joy'ſt the early walk to take
Where, thro' the pheaſant-haunted brake
Oft as the well-aim'd gun reſounds,
The eager-daſhing ſpaniel bounds.

For thee of Buck my breeches tight,
Clanging whip, and rowels bright,
The hunter's cap my brows to guard,
And ſuit of ſportive green's prepar'd:
For, ſince theſe delights are thine,
CHRISTMAS, with thy bands I join.

FREE IMITATION

OF

A LATIN ODE,

BY WALTER DE MAPES,

ARCHDEACON OF OXFORD IN THE ELEVENTH CENTURY.

L

CANTILENA.

Mihi est propositum in tabernâ mori,
Vinum sit appositum morentis ori,
Ut dicant, cùm venerint Angelorum chori:
" Deus sit propitius huic Potatori!"

Poculis accenditur animi lucerna;
Cor imbutum Nectare volat ad superna;
Mihi sapit dulcius vinum in tabernâ
Quàm quod aquâ miscuit præsulis Pincerna.

Suum cuique proprium dat Natura munus,
Ego nunquam potui scribere jejunus:
Me jejunum vincere posset puer unus,
Sitim et jejunium odi tanquam funus.

FREE IMITATION.

I'll in a tavern end my days 'midft boon companions merry,
Place at my lips a lufty flafk replete with fparkling fherry,
That angels hov'ring round may cry, when I lie dead as door-nail:
" Rife, genial Deacon, rife and drink of the Well of Life Eternal."

'Tis Wine the fading lamp of life renews with fire celeftial,
And elevates the raptur'd fenfe above this globe terreftrial;
Be mine the grape's pure juice unmix'd with any bafe ingredient,
Water to heretics I leave, found churchmen have no need on't.

Various implements belong to ev'ry occupation;
Give me an haunch of venifon,---and a fig for infpiration!
Verfes and odes without good cheer I never could indite 'em,
Sure he who Meager Days devis'd is d---d ad infinitum!

Tales verfus facio quale vinum bibo,
Non poffum fcribere nifi fumpto cibo;
Nihil valet penitùs quod jejunus fcribo,
Nafonem poft calices facilè præibo.

Mihi nunquàm fpiritus prophetiæ datur
Nifi cùm fuerit venter benè fatur;
Cùm in arce cerebri Bacchus dominatur
In me Phœbus irruit ac miranda fatur.

When I exhauſt the bowl profound and gen'rous liquor ſwallow,
Bright as the beverage I imbibe the gen'rous numbers follow;
Your ſneaking water-drinkers all, I utterly condemn 'em,
He that would write like Homer muſt drink like Agamemnon.

Myſteries and prophetic truths, I never could unfold 'em
Without a flagon of good wine and a ſlice of cold ham;
But when I've drain'd my liquor out, and eat what's in the diſh up,
Tho' I am but an Arch-deacon, I can preach like an Archbiſhop.

SONG.

To Chloe kind and Chloe fair,
With fparkling eye and flowing hair,
Tune the harp, and raife the fong;
Such as to Beauty doth belong!

Let the ftrain be fweet and clear;
Such as through the liftening ear,
In well-according harmony,
May with the 'tranced foul agree!

She is Pleafure's blooming Queen:
In the Morn more frefh her mien,
When awaken'd from repofe,
Than the fummer's dewy rofe:
In the Ev'ning brighter far
Than the ocean-bathed ftar.

    And when Night the friend of Love

Bids the filent hour improve,

To the ravifh'd fenfes SHE

Gives joy, and blifs, and ecttafy.

THE

RENOWNED HISTORY

AND

RARE ACHIEVEMENTS

OF

JOHN W****S.

AN HEROICK BALLAD.

DICERE RES GRANDES NOSTRO DAT MUSA POETÆ.

PERSIUS, SAT. I.

M

HEROICK BALLAD.

———————

FULL often I have read, inscrib'd
On parchment and on vellum,
The deeds of Ancient Heroes, and
The chances that befell 'em;
And ballads I have heard rehears'd
By harmonists itinerant,
Who Modern Worthies celebrate,
Yet scarcely make a dinner on't:
Some of whom sprang from noble race,
And some were in pigstye born;
Dependent upon Royal grace,
Or triple tree of Tyburn.
And sundry Gallants yet unsung,
Who scarcely have their fellows,
Amendments move in Parliament,
Or live by mending bellows:

But, of all who were or will be fung
In folemn ftave or ditty,
There's none can vie with JOHNNY W----s,
The C---------n of the City.

JOHN W----s he was for M-------x,
They chofe him Knight of the Shire:
And he made a Fool of Alderman B---,
And call'd Parfon H---- a Lyar.

Homer, for provender and fame
When he was blind and pennylefs,
Defcanted of the Spartan Dame,
Who a cuckold made of Menelaus:
His Heroes' founding names you've heard,
Whofe blood or brains were fpill'd in
Troy's fiege, as long as Neftor's beard
Which rooks their nefts did build in.

Virgil Æneas fung, of yore
Approv'd a valiant foldier,
Thro' flaughter, fmoke, and flame, he bore
His Dad upon his fhoulder:
(Elfe had fome fwaggering Grecian Boy
Soon made a hole in his fkin,
And fpitted him in burning Troy
To roaft like a pork grifkin.)
Æneas, hence, for piety
Was fam'd, or folks belie him;
Yet Helenus was as good as he,
And Chaplain to King Priam.
But why the merits do I vaunt
Of chaplain or of layman?
JOHN W----s is brave as John of Gaunt,
Religious as a Bramin:
Where wit or weapon came in play
Nothing for JOHN was too hard;
He wrote againft the KING all day,
And at night he fought HIS STEWARD.

Eke was he FRIAR OF MEDENHAM,
And liv'd in orthodoxy;
For, when he could not pray himfelf,
The MONKEY was his Proxy.

CHORUS.
JOHN W----s he was for M--------x, &c.

Old Shylock, the Jew-broker,
Was both covetous and cruel;
He hoarded up his ducats, and
He dined on watergruel;
And, when Anthonio could not pay
The monies he had borrow'd,
He pulled out his Snicker-fnee
With imprecations horrid:
" Thy bond is forfeited," he cried,
" The Penalty, I afk it;
" Ay, and a pound of Chriftian flefh
" I'll cut from thy bread-bafket."

But, when poor SYLVA JOHN befought
That he would but name his Pay-day,
JOHN fwore that he had no fuch word
In his Encylopedia:
Whereat this patient Ifraelite
He waxed wondrous ire:
But lo! JOHN chous'd him of his bond,
And he burnt it in the fire.

CHORUS.

JOHN W----s he was for M--------x, &c.

Fair Hannah Snell her farthingale
Pull'd off and, under cover
Of breeches and a foldier's coat,
Purfued her abfent lover:
Her bodkin, to a pike transform'd,
She brandifh'd in her right hand,
And Frenchmen's fouls thro' eyelet holes
I' their carcafes fhe frighten'd:

This female Mufqueteer her foes
As flat as flounders laid 'em ;
Powder and ball ferv'd her inftead
Of powder and pomatum.
Paris, for love of Helena,
Kindled a fierce combuftion ;
Confum'd in flames the town of Troy,
And Priam's breeches fuftian.
And great Alcides, fon of Jove,
Maugre his ftrength and valour,
For love of beauteous Omphale
Became a woman's taylor:
He, who th' Augëan ftables cleans'd,
A kerchief hemm'd to pleafe her:
Antæus once he fqueez'd to death,
But now became mop-fqueezer:
Yet all this he endur'd for Love,
And eke bore many an hard drub :
But for Love of Parfon H----'s lac'd coat
John ---ftole away his wardrobe.

CHORUS.

JOHN W----s he was for M-------x, &c.

Mahomet, marching at the head
Of his victorious rabble,
His apoftolic miffion prov'd
With fword irrefragable;
A Heaven of wine and women preach'd,
To make men more devout;
And if he could not turn their brains
His Saracens beat 'em out:
Gabriel took Mahomet to heav'n
And did a Mule provide him;
And thus JOHN W----s to Brentford rode
With Parfon H---- befide him:
There 'mongft the men of Middlefex
Renown and fame he got him,
And chofen was to mend the ftate,
Becaufe 'twas old and rotten;

N

And Ch--------n was after made
For 's juft and righteous dealings;
They wifely trufted to his charge
All their half-crowns and fhillings.
Then a fig for Mecca's Saint, a fig
For Tartar, Turk, or Saracen;
Our Ch-------n that rafcal-race
Excels beyond comparifon:
Their Founder was an arrant cheat;
JOHN W----s is no impoftor:
He cares no more for the Alcoran
Than for the Pater Nofter.

CHORUS.

JOHN W----s he was for M-------x, &c.

Renown'd in ancient ftory was
St. George, the Capadocian,
Whofe fpear, like Turkey-rhubarb, fet
The Dragon's guts in motion.

Achilles Hector did affail,
Transfix'd him with his javelin,
Then dragg'd him at his horfe's tail
Round every Trojan ravelin.
Ryance his mantle lined with beards
Of kings, inftead of ermine; k
And Arthur's royal chin to fhave
With 's broadfword did determine;
But Arthur quell'd the Welfhman's boaft,
He kill'd him dead as door-nail,
And fent him down his cheefe to toaft
At Pluto's fire infernal.
Intrepid Guy of Warwick to
A giant gave defiance;
Cut off his head and made him an
Example to all giants:
A fierce Dun Cow came in his way,
And on the head he knock'd her;
But valorous JOHN W----s, he cow'd
Sir William B--------p Pr-----r.

CHORUS.

JOHN W----s he was for M-------x, &c.

Your Oftrich, he will fwallow brafs,
And iron he loves dearly :
He'll pick up a peck of tenpenny nails
As cocks and hens do barley.
POWELL, as fome folks take fmall beer
To cool 'em when they have drank hard,
Steep'd in his brandy capficum,
Like burrage in cold-tankard :
And redhot coals, inftead of rolls,
Ate for his breakfaft duly,
Burnt brimftone, gunpowder, and pitch
To him were foup and bouillie :
Sky-rockets, 'ftead of faufages,
Ran hiffing down his weafen ;
Wafh'd down with aqua-fortis ftrong,
To keep his guts from freezing.

The Dragon of Wantley churches ate,

(He us'd to come on a Sunday)

Whole congregations were to him

A dish of Salmagundi:

He gave no quarter, no not he,

To clergymen or laymen:

Crack'd ev'n the Sexton's jobberknowl,

And fpoil'd him for faying Amen:

He pouch'd the Prebendaries all,

Who ne'er gave him an ill word;

Snapp'd up the Dean, as fnug in his ftall

As a maggot in a filbert.

The Corporation worfhipful

He valued not an ace,

But fwallow'd the Mayor, afleep in his chair,

And pick'd his teeth with the Mace.

He brows'd on monumental brafs

Fix'd in the walls o' th' cloyfters;

And fhoals of bawling chorifters

He ate, like fcallop'd oyfters.

He quarrell'd with the fteeple clock
And ate him while he was ftriking;
Bellropes he munch'd for chitterlings,
Tho' they wer'n't fo much to his liking:
Tombftones and monuments he took
For pills to cool his palate;
And cropt the church yard yew-trees all---
They ferv'd him for a fallad.
The organ that fo loud did roar
Devour'd he in his frolick;
And batten'd on the bellows-blower,
For he fear'd not the wind-colick.
To fcape his facrilegious maw
This Dragon he gave none chance,
But fwallow'd the knave that fet the ftave,
And felt no qualm of confcience:
Parfons were his black-puddings, and
Fat Aldermen his capons;
And his tid-bit the Collection Plate
Brimful of Birmingham halfpence.

Clerks, Curates, Rectors, Bifhops ate
This Dragon moft uncivil;
And (but he never comes to church)
He would have ate the D---l.
But the Men of Aylefbury efteem
John W----s a greater rarity:
They made Him Truftee for their School,
And He fwallow'd up the Charity.

CHORUS.

John W----s he was for M-------x,
They chofe him Knight of the Shire:
And he made a Fool of Alderman B---,
And call'd Parfon H---- a Liar.

SONG

ON THE BREAKING OF THE WATER-HEAD, NEAR
WINDSOR GREAT PARK,
COMMONLY CALLED, THE POND-HEAD.

———————

When *** was employ'd to conſtruct the Pond Head,
As he ponder'd the taſk, to himſelf thus he ſaid:
" Since a head I muſt make, what's a head but a noddle?
" So I think I had beſt take My Own for a model."

Derry down, &c.

Then his work our Projector began out of hand,
The outſide he conſtructed with rubbiſh and ſand,
But brains on this Head had been quite thrown away,
Thoſe he kept for himſelf, ſo he lined it with clay.

O

An head thus compacted and well put together
Bade defiance he thought both to water and weather,
With profound admiration must strike all beholders,
And surpass ev'ry head except that on his shoulders.

The fam'd Friar Bacon he 'counted an ass,
Tho' the head that He made was a blockhead of brass;
And he little suspected it e'er should be said,
That himself all this while was not right in his head.

But the water at length, to his utter dismay,
A Bankruptcy made, and his head ran away;
'Twas a thick head for certain; but, had it been thicker,
No head can endure that is always in liquor.

It was owing no doubt to some Capital error,
That one Broken Head struck the country with terror;

And 'twas well for the folks whom this deluge furrounded
That, born to be hang'd, there were none of them drowned.

Trump's Mill in the Bottom was never fupplied,
Since firft it went round, with fo plenteous a tide;
Yet the Miller he wifh'd that our head-maker's fkill
Lefs water had fent and more grift to his mill.

Our Projector, in truth, left him little to brag on
When his meal-facks march'd off without horfes or waggon;
And to refcue himfelf he muft fain ftir his ftumps:
Such an odd trick was play'd on this Miller of Trump's!

Yet ❁ ❁ ❁ full as ill as the Miller has fped,
And atones for his fault with the lofs of his Head:
Tho' fome folks will tell you, (believe 'em who lift)
Long ago had he loft it, 't would ne'er have been mifs'd.

Now, although I muſt own 'tis a difficult caſe
In diſcuſſing this head to preſerve a grave face,
More compaſſion its Maker may challenge than ſatire,
Since 'tis plain that he can't keep his head above water.

This at leaſt may be urg'd in his favour I deem;
His is not the firſt head which has gone with the ſtream:
And---as for his Honour---'tis ſafe you may ſwear,
Since Butler has told us That lodges elſewhere.[1]

Hence, by way of a Moral, the fallacy's ſhewn
Of the maxim that Two Heads are better than One:
For none e'er was ſo ſcurvily dealt with before,
By the Head that he made and the Head that he wore.

Derry down, &c.

WILLIAM OF WICKHAM,

A SONG,

FOR THE WICCAMICAL ANNIVERSARY, HELD AT THE
CROWN AND ANCHOR TAVERN.

I SING not your heroes of ancient romance:
Capadocian George, or Saint Denis of France;
   No chronicler I am
   Of Troy and King Priam,
And thofe crafty old Greeks who to fritters did fry 'em:
But your voices, Brave Boys, one and all I befpeak 'em,
In due celebration of William of Wickham.

CHORUS.

Let Wickham's Brave Boys, at the Crown and the Anchor,
The flafk never quit 'till clean out they have drank her;
And united maintain, whether fober or mellow,
That old Billy Wickham was a Very Fine Fellow.

The fwain who in amorous fervitude glories
Swears that Love builds his neft in the eyebrow of Chloris,
    While fhafts from the quiver
    Of that Urchin Deceiver,
Like the quills of a porcupine, ftick in his liver:
But at Wickham's Brave Boys fhould he brandifh his dart,
We'll drown the Blind Rogue in a Winchefter Quart.

CHORUS.

For Wickham's Brave Boys, &c.

Let fomenters of fierce Oppofition exclaim
That our rulers are blind and our politics lame;
    While their fole aim and wifh is,
    With loaves and with fifhes
From the Treafury Board to replenifh their difhes:
How fuch Orators fare, my Boys, who cares a button,
While We have good Claret and Winchefter Mutton!

CHORUS.

For Wickham's Brave Boys, &c.

Let the Soldier, who prates about ftorming the trenches

Of fortified towns, and of fair-vifag'd wenches,

My numbers give heed to,

And, drinking as we do,

Shut up in its fcabbard his martial Toledo:

For we too fhed blood, yet all danger efcape,

Since the blood that we fhed is the blood of the Grape.

CHORUS.

Let Wickham's Brave Boys, &c.

Let Lawyers, accuftom'd to quarrel and brawl,

Play the devil as ufual in Weftminfter Hall;

Reputations befpatter,

Yet thrive and grow fatter,

While they dafh Wrong and Right up as cookmaids do Batter:

Here good fellowfhip reigns and, what's ftranger by far,

No mifchief enfues from a Call to the Bar.

CHORUS.

Let Wickham's Brave Boys, &c.

The Empiric profound, who in heathenish Latin
Such potions prescribes as might poison old Satan,
  With blister and bolus
  And draught would cajole us,
'Till snug under ground he has clapt in a hole us:
But the wise Sons of Wickham his regimen slight,
They swallow no draughts but of Red Wine and White.

CHORUS.

  Let Wickham's Brave Boys, &c.

Ye Poetical Tribe, on Parnaffus who forage,
Who prate of Jove's Nectar and Helicon-porridge,
  Yet, for beef-steaks and brandy,
  Set each Jack-a-dandy
On a level with Frederick, or Prince Ferdinandy:
What's the sword of King Arthur or Admiral Hosier
To William of Wickham and his Jolly Old Crosier!

CHORUS.

Let Wickham's Brave Boys at the Crown and the Anchor, &c.

THE BARBER'S NUPTIALS.

QUI FACERE ASSUERAT----
CANDIDA DE NIGRIS.   OVID MET.

In Liquorpond Street, as is well known to many,
An artift refided who fhav'd for a penny,
Cut hair for three halfpence, for three pence he bled,
And would draw for a groat ev'ry tooth in your head.

What annoy'd other folks never fpoil'd his repofe,
'Twas the fame thing to him whether ftocks fell or rofe,
For blaft and for mildew he car'd not a pin;
His Crops never fail'd, for they grew on the Chin.

Unvex'd by the cares that ambition and ftate has,
Contented he dined on his daily potatoes;

P

And the pence that he earn'd by excifion of briftle
Were nightly devoted to whetting his whiftle.

When copper ran low he made light of the matter,
Drank his purl upon tick at the Old Pewter Platter,[m]
Read the News, and as deep in the Secret appear'd
As if he had lather'd the Minifter's beard.

But Cupid, who trims men of every ftation,
And 'twixt barbers and beaux makes no difcrimination;
Would not let this fuperlative Shaver alone,
'Till he tried if his heart was as hard as his hone.

The Fair One, whofe charms did the Barber enthral,
At the end of Fleet Market of Fifh kept a ftall:
As red as her cheek no boil'd lobfter was feen,
Not an eel that fhe fold was as foft as her fkin.

By love ftrange effects have been wrought, we are told,

In all countries and climates, hot, temperate, and cold;

Thus the heart of our Barber love fcorch'd to a coal,

Tho' 'tis very well known he liv'd under the Pole.

Firft, he courted his charmer in forrowful fafhion,

And lied, like a lawyer, to move her compaffion:

He fhould perifh, he fwore, did his fuit not fucceed,

And a Barber to flay was a barbarous deed.

Then he alter'd his tone and was heard to declare,

If valour deferv'd the regard of the Fair,

That his courage was tried, tho' he fcorn'd to difclofe

How many brave fellows he'd took by the nofe.

For his politics too, they were thoroughly known,

A patriot he was to the very back bone;

WILKES he gratis had ſhav'd, for the good of the nation,
And he held the WHIG CLUB in profound veneration.

For his tenets religious, he well could expound
Emanuel Sweedenbourg's myſt'ries profound,
And new doctrines could broach with the beſt of 'em all,
For a perriwig - maker ne'er wanted a Caul.

Thus this Knight of the Baſon confounded together
Courage, politics, love, inſpiration, and lather:
But his hard-hearted miſtreſs, ſhe ſet him at nought;
No gudgeon was ſhe, nor ſo eaſily caught.

Indignant ſhe anſwer'd: " No chin-ſcraping ſot
" Shall be faſten'd to me by the conjugal knot,
" No!---to Tyburn repair, if a nooſe you muſt tie,
" Other fiſh I have got, Mr. Tonſor, to fry.

" Holborn-bridge and Black Friars my triumphs can tell,

" From Bilingſgate Beauties I've long borne the bell:

" Nay, tripemen and fiſhmongers vie for my favour---

" Then d'ye think I'll take up with a Twopenny Shaver?

" Let dory, or turbot, the ſov'reign of fiſh,

" Cheek by jowl with red herring be ſerv'd in one diſh;

" Let ſturgeon and ſprats in one pickle unite,

" When I angle for huſbands and Barbers ſhall bite."

But the Barber perſiſted (Ah, could I relate 'em!)

To ply her with compliments ſoft as pomatum;

And took ev'ry occaſion to flatter and praiſe her,

Till ſhe fancied his wit was as keen as his razor.

He proteſted beſides, if ſhe'd grant his petition,

She ſhould live like a lady of rank and condition:

And to Bilingſgate market no longer repair,
But himſelf all her bus'neſs would do to a hair.

Her ſmiles, he aſſerted, would melt even rocks,
Nay the fire of her eyes would conſume barbers' blocks,
On inſenſible objects beſtow animation,
And give to old perriwigs regeneration.

With fair ſpeeches cajol'd, as you'd tickle a trout,
'Gainſt the Barber the Fiſhwife no more could hold out ;
He applied the right bait, and with flattery he caught her ;
Without flattery a female 's a fiſh out of water.

The ſtate of her heart when the Barber once gueſs'd
Love's ſiege with redoubled exertion he preſs'd ;
And as briſkly beſtirr'd him, the charmer embracing,
As the waſhball that dances and froths in his baſon.

The flame to allay that their bofoms did fo burn,
They fet out for the church of St. Andrew in Holborn,
Where tonfors and trulls, country Dicks and their coufins,
In the halter of wedlock are tied up by dozens.

The Nuptials to grace came from every quarter
The worthies at Rag Fair old caxons who barter,
Who the coverings of judges and counfellors' nobs
Cut down into majors, queues, fcratches, and bobs.

Mufclemongers and oyftermen, crimps, and coalheavers,
And butchers with marrowbones fmiting their cleavers;
Shrimpfcalders and bugkillers, taylors and tylers,
Boys, botchers, bawds, bailiffs, and blackpudding-boilers.

From their voices united fuch melody flow'd
As the Abbey ne'er witnefs'd, nor Tott'nham Court Road:

While Saint Andrew's brave bells did fo loud and fo clear ring,
You'd have given ten pounds to 've been out of their hearing.

For his fee---when the Parfon this couple had join'd,
As no cafh was forth-coming, he took it in kind:
So the Bridegroom difmantled his Rev'rence's chin,
And the Bride entertain'd him with pilchards and gin.

THE CLIMAX.

BEFORE I came to London
I us'd to sip TEA with my Mother,
  And I thought it a treat
  If SMALL-BEER I could get
To drink with my Elder Brother.

      Tol-de-rol, &c.

But my Father condemn'd this practice,
He hector'd and swore like mad---Sir:
  Says he, " Give him ALE,
  " For that will never fail
" To make him as stout as his Dad---Sir."

Q

Soon after, our Ned the Butler
Took me down to tafte fome October:---
 Cried he, " Never fear
 " To drink STRONG-BEER,
" But fwallow it, drunk or fober.

But when I arriv'd in London
Of PORTER I drank my pot---Sir,
 A pipe did I funk,
 And fo oft got drunk
That my Sifter call'd me a Sot---Sir.

From Beer to WINE I afcended
By a feries of juft gradation:
 'Till my friends would me jog
 With---" There's a jolly Dog
" Soon fhall tope with the beft of the nation."

With a Blood then I got acquainted,
Who ſtrait prov'd wond'rous handy:
 For he taught me to ſwear
 Like a Grenadier;
And always drink RUM or BRANDY.

Thus I to Drams betook me,
And Wine I drank no longer:
 Sometimes I threw in
 GUNPOWDER to my GIN,
To make the potion ſtronger.

But, conſidering all things earthly,
That the ſpan of Life ſo ſhort is:---
 Whate'er you may think,
 I ſtill ſhall drink
Till I come to AQUA-FORTIS.
      Tol-de-roll, &c.

A MORSEL FOR A MUSSULMAN:

OR

A REVELATION OF THE FUTURE STATE OF DECEASED FEMALES,

IN REFUTATION OF THE SUPPOSED MAHOMETAN DOCTRINE, ASSERTING THAT WOMEN HAVE NO SOULS, AND ARE EXCLUDED FROM PARADISE.

―― NON ME IMPIA NAMQUE
TARTARA HABENT TRISTESQUE UMBRÆ: SED AMÆNA――
CONCILIA ELYSIUMQUE COLO.――

VIRG. ÆN. L. 5.

From the bleſt realms where Paradiſe diſplays
Her empyrëan ſplendour's ceaſeleſs blaze,
And bids her groves of vegetable gold
To genial gales immortal blooms unfold;
From nectar'd ſtreams where Houris, heavenly-fair,
Bathe the bright treſſes of their odorous hair.

To Zeyneib, lovelieſt of the paſſive train
That 'midſt the Haram's hated glooms complain,
Alzira's happy Shade appearing, ſteals
A pauſe from bliſs, and thus her ſtate reveals:

" Say to the tyrant Man, whoſe pride denies
" Thy ſex a Soul, and bars them from the ſkies,
" That when the date of female worth expires,
" And ſickening Nature yields her lateſt fires,
" When beams no more the luſtre of the eye,
" And death o'er beauty hails his victory,
" To life by Fate recall'd, the Sex aſſume
" Celeſtial charms, and never-fading bloom;
" In roſeate bowers recline, or bliſsful rove
" Thro' ſcenes of boundleſs joy and rapturous love;
" That there, ſo Heaven ordains, a blooming band
" Of Youths, obſequious to each Fair's command,
" Attentive waits, and, as her fancy wills,
" Each taſk of duty or of love fulfills.---

" Then to the peremptory Tyrant fay,

" Who hopes this lot in Heaven muſt Here obey,

" Bow to fuperior worth, to fenfe refin'd,

" Blefs the benignant fway of Womankind,

" Hail the fair Fabrick of an Hand Divine,

" And own the Soul that animates the Shrine.---

" Or, driven for ever from the realms above,

" His Soul in vain ſhall pant for Heavenly Love."

THE PARADOX:

OR

NED FRIGHTENED OUT OF HIS WITS.

E<small>MPTY</small> the flaſk, diſcharg'd the ſcore,
N<small>ED</small> ſtagger'd from the tavern door,
And, falling in his drunken fits,
Crippled his Noſe and loſt his Wits;
But, from the kennel ſoon emerging,
His noſe repairs by help of ſurgeon:
That done, the Leech peeps in his brain
To find his wits,---but peeps in vain.
" 'Tis hard," the Patient cries, " to loſe
" Wits not a whit the worſe for uſe;
" Wits which I always laid aſide
" For great occaſions, cut and dried;"
('Tho' here the caſe was falſely put:
His Wits were dried, Himſelf was Cut.)
" Wits like the Continental Aloe,
" That for a century lies fallow;

" Wits never prodigally wafted;
" Like choice conferves, but rarely tafted:
" Wits hufbanded, not fpent at random ;
" Cork'd up like cordials for my Grandam:
" Wits, which, if all your wealth could buy---Sir,
" You would not be a jot the wifer."

Tho' plain appear'd in ev'ry face
A fellow-feeling of his cafe,
Yet ftill, to fhew Their Wits were found,
Ilis Boon Companions throng around,
And fagely, one and all, accoft him:
" Zounds, NED, I wonder how you loft 'em!"

Ah! let them drink their Port in peace,
For miracles will never ceafe!
And, if NED'S LOSS OF WITS aftound 'em,
Zounds,---how they'll wonder when HE'S FOUND 'EM!

ADDRESS

OF AN INDIAN GIRL TO AN ADDER.

WRITTEN IN THE YEAR 1740.

BY AN EMINENT LITERARY CHARACTER, THEN A SCHOLAR
OF WINCHESTER COLLEGE.

STAY, ſtay, thou lovely fearful Snake!
Nor hide thee in yon darkſome brake;
But let me oft thy form review,
Thy ſparkling eyes, and golden hue:
From thence a chaplet ſhall be wove
To grace the youth I deareſt love.

Then, ages hence, when Thou no more
Shalt glide along the ſunny ſhore,
Thy copied beauties ſhall be ſeen;
Thy vermeil red and living green
In mimic folds thou ſhalt diſplay:
Stay, lovely, fearful ADDER, ſtay!

R

EPITAPHIUM SUSANNAE SERLE,

IN ECCLESIA DE TESTWOOD, IN COMITATU HANT:

CONJUX chara Vale!---Tibi, Maritus,
Hoc pono memori manu fepulchrum:
At quales lacrymas Tibi rependam,
Dum trifti recolo, Sufanna, corde
Quàm conftans, animo neque impotente,
Tardi fuftuleras acuta lethi,
Me fpectans placidis fupremum ocellis!---
Quòd fi pro meritis vel Ipfe flerem,
Quo fletu tua Te relicta Proles,
Proles parvula, ritè profequetur
Cuftodem, fociam, ducem, parentem!
At quorsùm lachrymæ?---Valeto, raræ
Exemplum pietatis, O Sufanna!

LINES

ON THE LATE AMERICAN WAR.

WRITTEN IN THE YEAR 1778.

———

Upon a treſtle Pig was laid,
And a ſad ſquealing ſure It made;
Kill-pig ſtood by with knife and ſteel:
" Lie quiet, can't you?---Why d'ye ſqueal?
" Have I not fed you with my Peaſe,
" And now, for trifles ſuch as theſe,
" Will you rebel?---Brimful of victual,
" Won't you be kill'd and cur'd a little?"
To whom thus Piggy in reply:
" Think'ſt thou that I ſhall quiet lie,
" And that for Pease my Life I'll barter?"---
" Then Piggy, you muſt ſhew your Charter;
" Shew You 're exempted more than Others,
" Elſe go to pot like all your brothers.---

[PIG STRUGGLES.

" Help, Neighbours! help!---this PIG 's fo ftrong,

" I think I cannot hold him long.

" Help, Neighbours! I can't keep him under!

" Where are ye all?---See, by your blunder,

" He 's burft his cords!---A brute uncivil,

" He 's gone!---I'll after---

[Exit PIG, and KILL-PIG after him with the KNIFE, &c.

CHORUS OF NEIGHBOURS.

To the Devil!

EXTEMPORE

ON A SNARLING AGENT OF LORD A✸✸✸✸✸✸✸✸'S, AT
WHITEHAM, NEAR OXFORD.

I am his Lordfhip's DOG at Whiteham,
And whom he bids me bite, I bite 'em.

EPIGRAMMATA.

IN SOMNIS VIDERAT HERMOGENEM.

REGES occidunt verbis, basiliscus ocello,
Aëre desævit pestis, et ore leo:
Esse tamen Medicis propiora negotia Fati
Creditur, UMBRA eadem est MORTIS et HERMOGENIS.

LONGA DIES IGITUR QUID CONTULIT?

LONGA DIES igitur quid contulit, Optime, quæris?
NOCTEM, ni fallor, contulit ille BREVEM.

IN TONSOREM VERSIFICANTEM.

Quid TIBI cum PHÆBO?---non est BARBATUS Apollo.

EPITAPHIUM JUVENIS QUI PROPTER AMOREM
"MOLLY STONE" MORTEM SIBI CONSCIVIT.

MOLLY fuit Saxum; fi Saxum MOLLE fuiffet
Non foret Hic fubtùs, fed fupereffet Eam.

IN ILLUSTRISSIMAM DOMINAM --------
IN AGRO BLENH------- Ἐπερύσαν.

Salve! Regia Virgo, quæ recenti
Largè noftra rigas vireta rivo!---
O, quæ tam benè mingis et benignè,
Vero nomine dicta PRINCIPISSA!

EPIGRAMS.

ON A FAVOURITE DOG, WHO REGULARLY ACCOMPANIED HIS MISTRESS TO CHURCH.

'Tis held by folks of deep refearch,
He 's a GOOD DOG who goes to Church:
As good I hold Him every whit
Who ftays at home and turns the Spit.
For, 'though GOOD DOGS to Church may go,
Yet going There don't make them fo.

While DICK to Combs hoftility proclaims,
A neighbouring taper fets his hair in flames.---
The blaze extinct, permit us to inquire:
" Were there no Lives loft, RICHARD, in THIS FIRE?"

IGNOTUM OMNE PRO MAGNIFICO.

Averfe to pamper'd and high-mettled fteeds,
His Own upon chopt Straw AVARO feeds:
Bred in His ftable, in His paddock born,
What vaft ideas They muft have of Corn!

———————

A CASE OF CONSCIENCE;

SUBMITTED TO A LATE DIGNITARY OF THE CHURCH,

ON

HIS NARCOTICK EXPOSITION OF THE FOLLOWING TEXT:

" WATCH AND PRAY, LEST YE ENTER INTO TEMPTATION."

By our PASTOR perplext,
How fhall we determine?---
" Watch and Pray," fays the TEXT,
" Go to fleep," fays the SERMON.

MONODY

ON

THE DEATH OF DICK,

AN ACADEMICAL CAT.

——— ——— MICAT INTER OMNES.

HOR. LIB. I. ODE 12.

S

MONODY

ON

THE DEATH OF DICK.

Ye Rats, in triumph elevate your ears!
Exult, ye Mice!---for Fate's abhorred shears
Of Dick's nine lives have slit the Catguts nine;
Henceforth he mews 'midst choirs of Cats divine!
Tho' nine successive lives protract their date,
E'en Cats themselves obey the call of Fate;
Whose formidable Fiat sets afloat
Mortals, and mortal Cats, in Charon's boat:
Fate, who Cats, Dogs, and Doctors makes his prize,
That grace Great Britain's Universities.

Where were ye, Nymphs,---when to the silent coast
Of gloomy Acheron Dick travell'd post?

Where were ye, Mufes, in that deathful hour?---
Say, did ye haunt the Literary Bower
Where Science fends her Sons in Stockings Blue
To barter praife for foup with M✿✿✿✿✿✿?
Or Point prepare for B✿✿✿✿✿✿'s Anecdote,
Or Songs infpire, and fit 'em to His Throat?---
For not on Isis' claffic fhores ye ftray'd,
Nor brew'd with Cherwell's wave your lemonade;
Nor affignations kept with Grizzled Elves,
Where Learning fleeps on Bodley's groaning fhelves;
Nor, where no poet glows with kindred fire,
Wept o'er your favourite Warton's filent Lyre.

While venal Cats (leagued with degenerate Curs,
Of faded Prudes the four-legg'd penfioners)
On the foft Sofa rang'd in order due,
For eleemofynary muffin mew,
Regardlefs of the meed that Fame beftows,
Their tail a feather for each wind that blows;

Thee, generous Dick, the Cat-controlling Powers
Ordain'd to moufe in Academic Bowers:
Bade Thee the facred ftreams of Sapience fip,
And in Piërean Cream thy whifkers dip!

Enfhrined celeftial Cateries among,
The fable Matron, from whofe loins he fprung,
Who traced her high defcent through ages dark
From Cats that Caterwaul'd in Noah's Ark,
Stern, brindled nurfe, with unremitting care,
To high achievements train'd her Tabby Heir;
On Patriot Cats his young attention fix'd,
And many a cuff with grave inftruction mix'd;
Taught the great Truth, to half his race unknown:
" Cats are not kitten'd for themfelves alone;
But hold from Heav'n their delegated claws,
Guardians of Larders, Liberty, and Laws."

" Let Cats and Catlings of ignoble line

" Slumber in bee-hive chairs, in dairies dine;

" Shun, Thou, the shades of Cat-enfeebling Ease!

" Watch o'er the weal of Rhedycinian cheese;

" The melting marble of Collegiate Brawn

" For Heads of Houses guard, and Lords in Lawn;

" And keep each recreant rat and mouse in awe

" That dares to shew his nose in GOLGOTHA."

" So may the brightest honours of the Gown

" Thy riper years and active virtue crown!---

" Say, shall not Cats, fraught with ethereal fire, °

" To feats of letter'd eminence aspire?---

" Caligula a conful made his Steed;

" What tho' the beast could neither write nor read,

° Yet could he Talents Negative display,

" And silence Opposition with his Neigh.

" If Charles of Sweden swore he would depute,

" The senate to control, his old Jack Boot;

" If modern taste a LEARNED PIG reveres,

" And Pigs unlearn'd keep company with PEERS; P

THE DEATH OF DICK.

" If erſt Rome's papal crown a Goſſip wore,
" Then, DICK, Thou may'ſt become Vicech-------r.

   " Might I but live, tho' crazy, old, and ſick,
" To ſee thee ſtalk behind thy Beadles, DICK !
" Behold my brindled boy with conſcious pride
" O'er convocated Grizzle-Wigs preſide!
" Hear thee, e'er I explore my lateſt home,
" Confer Degrees in SHELDON's ſpacious Dome!
" See thee in ſcarlet robe encaſe thy fur,
" And at St. MARYS' venerably purr!---
" Then let me be tranſlated to the ſkies,
" And cloſe in welcome death theſe gooſeb'ry eyes!

   " Yet think not, Darling DICK, that Fame allows
" Her glorious palm, unearn'd, to grace thy brows:
" By toil Herculean and profound reſearch
" Expect to thrive in Politicks or Church!

" The herd who worſhip at Preferment's ſhrine
" No ſervile taſk, no ſacriſice, decline;
" Courtiers for coronets their conſcience pawn,
" Clerks in Prunello creep, then ſoar in Lawn,
" See, with the Ribband grac'd and radiant Star,
" The Chief that waged the Continental War!
" Such palms diminiſh'd realms can yet afford
" To patriotic H***'s protracting Sword!
" See W****s, untruſted with the CITY KEY
" Till he made fools of all the Livery!
" See grov'ling S**** the wealth of India ſhare:
" He taught the Hindù Race to feed on air!

" Mark the career of Rhedycina's Bard;---
" Not ſuch His Toil, not ſuch His Vaſt Reward.
" Glean'd from Antiquity's exhauſtleſs mine,
" He bade the gems of Science brighter ſhine;
" His care retriev'd each venerable name
" Reft by Oblivion from the rolls of Fame,

" And with new glory crown'd the Strains fublime

" That echoed from the Harps of elder time.

" 'Twas his, 'midft mouldering palms of Chivalry,

" To braid the deathlefs blooms of Poefy ;

" On learning's gloom the rays of Tafte to pour,

" And gild with genuine Wit the focial hour ;

" Affection and applaufe alike he fhar'd ;

" All lov'd the Man, all venerate the Bard :

" Ev'n Prejudice his fate afflicted hears,

" And Letter'd Envy fheds reluctant tears.---

" Of genius, tafte, philanthrophy, and fenfe,

" Candour, and wit---behold the Recompenfe !

" No Sinecure, no venerable Stall,

" He fills, o'ercanopied with crimfon pall ;

" No Choir obfequious waits his dread commands,

" Where fupple Vergers pace with filver wands ;

" Where foft reclines in velvet pomp fupreme

" DIVINITY, entranc'd in mitrous dream :

T

" No Coin his meed---for claffic fobs unfit---
" For, ah! what fellowfhip has Wealth with Wit!
" Such worth THE LAUREL could alone repay,
" Profan'd by CIBBER, and contemn'd by GRAY; ¶
" Yet hence its Wreath fhall new diftinction claim,
" And, tho' it gave not, take from WARTON fame."

While glory's fteep afcent GRIMALKIN fhews,
DICK's breaft with emulative ardour glows;
His emerald eyes with richer radiance roll,
And ALL THE CAT awakens in his foul.
Within the tender velvet of his paw
Tho' yet unbloodied lurks each virgin claw;
Anticipated palms his hope defcries,
And conquefts gain'd o'er vifionary mice:
Tho' much for Milk, more for Renown he mews,
And nobler objects than his Tail purfues.

O, could I call the Mufes from the fpheres
To fing the triumphs of his riper years!
What ftrife the larder's confcious fhelves beheld!
What congregated rats his valour quell'd!
What mice defcended, at each direful blow,
To nibble brimftone in the realms below!---
The Victor, who his foes in furious mood
Hurl'd from the Granic to the Stygian flood;
Churchill, whofe bounty fainting Frenchmen gave
Soup-meagre gratis in the Danube's wave;
Heathfield, whofe red-hot vengeance Spain defied,
Blift'ring, like Spanifh flies, Old Neptune's hide;
Who plung'd his enemies, a whifker'd group,
In green waves twice as hot as green peas foup,
While Fate on Calpe's fummit fat and fmil'd
To fee the dingy Dons like lobfters boil'd,
Or by the light'ning of th' exploded fhell
Difpatch'd to feek a cooler birth in Hell---
All Heroes, bloody, brave, or politic,
All, all fhould yield preeminence to DICK:

And everlasting laurels, thick as hops,
Wreath their bright foliage round his brindled chops.

Mysterious Powers, who rule the destinies
Of conquerors and kings, of cats and mice,
Why did your will the Pylian Chief decree
Three centuries unspectacled to see,
Yet summon from his patriot toils away
Illustrious Dick, before his beard was grey?
Of valour, sense, or skill, how vain the boast!---
Dick seeks the shades, an undistinguish'd Ghost,
And turns his tail on this terrestrial ball,
Dismiss'd without Mandamus Medical;
Sent, without purge or Catapotium,
In prime of Cat-hood to the Catacomb;
No Doctor fee'd, no regimen advis'd,
Unpill'd, unpoultic'd, unphlebotomiz'd!

Ye fage Divines, if fo concife our fpan,
Who for preferment would turn Cat in pan?
Since Clergymen and Cats one fate betides,
And worms fhall eat their fermons and their hides!

Polecats, who DICK's difaftrous end furvive,
Shall blefs their ftars that they ftill ftink alive;
Mufkcats fhall feel a melancholy qualm,
And with their fweets departed DICK embalm;
Cats in each clime and latitude that dwell,
Brown, fable, fandy, grey, and tortoifefhell,
Of titles obfolete, or yet in ufe,
Tom, Tybert, Roger, Rutterkin[r], or Pufs;
Cats who with wayward Hags the moon control,
Unchain the winds, and bid the thunders roll;
Brave in enchanted fieves the boift'rous main,
And Royal barks with adverfe blafts detain;[s]
Nay Two-legg'd Cats, as well as Cats with four,
Shall DICK's irreparable lofs deplore.

Cats who frail nymphs in gay affemblies guard,
As buckram ftiff, and bearded like the pard;
Calumnious Cats who circulate faux pas,
And reputations maul with murd'rous claws;
Shrill Cats whom fierce domeftic brawls delight,
Crofs Cats who nothing want but teeth to bite,
Starch Cats of puritanic afpect fad,
And learned Cats who talk their hufbands mad;
Confounded Cats who cough, and croak, and cry,
And maudlin Cats who drink eternally;
Prim Cats of countenance and mien precife,
Yet oft'ner hankering for men than mice;
Curft Cats whom nought but caftigation checks,
Penurious Cats who buy their coals by pecks,
Faftidious Cats who pine for coftly Cates,
And jealous Cats who Catechife their mates;
Cat-Prudes who, when they're afk'd the queftion, fquall,
And ne'er give anfwer Categorical;

Uncleanly Cats who never pare their nails,
Cat-Goffips full of Canterbury tales,
Cat-Grandams vex'd with afthmas and Catarrhs,
And fuperftitious Cats who curfe their ftars;
Cats who their favours barter for a bribe,
And canting Cats, the worft of all the tribe!
And faded Virgin-Cats, and Tabbies old,
Who at quadrille remorfelefs moufe for gold;
Cats of each clafs, craft, calling, and degree
Mourn DICK's calamitous Cataftrophe.

Yet, while I chant the caufe of RICHARD's End,
Ye fympathizing Cats, your tears fufpend!
Then fhed enough to float a dozen whales,
And ufe, for pocket-handkerchiefs, your tails!---

Fame fays, (but Fame a fland'rer ftands confefs'd,)
DICK his own fprats, like B****R G********E, drefs'd:

But to the Advocates of Truth 'tis known,
He neither ſtaid for Grace nor Gridiron.
Raw ſprats he ſwore were worth all fiſh beſide,
Freſh, ſtale, ſtew'd, ſpitchcock'd, fricaſſee'd or fried;
Then ſwallow'd down a ſcore without remorſe,
And three fat Mice flew for his ſecond courſe:
But, while the third his grinders dyed with gore,
Sudden thoſe grinders clos'd---to grind no more!
And (dire to tell!) commiſſion'd by Old Nick,
A Catalepſy made an end of DICK.

Thus from the Paſty's furious eſcalade,
Where blood, to gravy turn'd, embrown'd his blade,
(That all-encount'ring blade which ſcorn'd to fear
Broil'd Gizzards charg'd with Kian-gunpowder)
From Rais'd-cruſt levell'd, never more to riſe,
From Ducks diſpatch'd, and maſſacred Minc'd-pies,
From Turkey-poults transfix'd and Sirloins flaſh'd,
From Marrow-puddings maul'd, and Cuſtards quaſh'd,

Crimpt Cod, and mutilated Mackarel,
And defolation of the Turtle's fhell,
Some Alderman, of giant appetite,
A furfeit fweeps to everlafting night:
Imbibing Claret with his latelt breath,
And brandifhing his knife and fork in death,
Downward a gormandizing gholt he goes,
And bears to Hell frefh fuel on his nofe;
For Calipafh explores th' infernal fcene, ᵗ
And wifhes Phlegethon one valt Terrene.

O Paragon of Cats, whofe lofs diftracts
My foul, and turns my tears to Cataracts,
Nor craft nor courage could thy doom prorogue!
DICK, premier Cat upon the Catalogue
Of Cats that grace a Caterwauling age,
Scar'd by Fate's Cat-call quits this earthly ftage;
Dire fled the arrow that laid RICHARD flat,
And fickening Glory faw Death fhoot a Cat.

Ah! tho' thy buſt adorn no ſculptur'd ſhrine,
No Vaſe thy relics, DICK, to fame conſign,
No rev'rend characters thy rank expreſs,
Nor hail thee, DICK, D. D. nor F. R. S.,
For Thee, 'midſt golden groves of Paradiſe,
Shall bloom the deathleſs wreath that Earth denies.
There, while GRIMALKIN'S mew her RICHARD greets,
A thouſand Cats ſhall purr on ſainted ſeats:
E'en now I ſee, deſcending from his throne,
Thy venerable Cat, O Whittington,
The kindred excellence of RICHARD hail,
And ſwell with joy his gratulating tail!
There ſhall the worthies of the Whiſker'd Race
Elyſian Mice o'er floors of ſapphire chaſe,
Midſt beds of aromatic marum ſtray,
Or raptur'd rove beſide the Milky Way.
Kittens, than Eaſtern Houris fairer ſeen,
Whoſe bright eyes gliſten with immortal green,

Shall fmooth for Tabby Swains their yielding fur,

And to their amorous Mews affenting purr.---

There, like Alcmena's, fhall GRIMALKIN's SON

In blifs repofe,---his moufing labours done,

Fate, Envy, Curs, Time, Tide and Traps defy,

And Caterwaul to all eternity.

EXPLANATORY NOTES.

(a) St. Leonard's Hill, in Windsor Forest, the residence of the Honourable General Harcourt.

(b) Cartoon.—The Death of Ananias, in the Royal Apartments at Windsor Castle.

(c) Cartoon.—Paul preaching at Athens.

(d) Cartoon.—Paul and Barnabas at Lystra.

(e) The Victories of Edward the Third, and Edward the Black Prince painted by Mr. West.

(f) "Morning.—The Season Winter. Cold as it may appear to be, we
"have here an Old Maid, going to seven o'clock Prayers, with her half-
"starved, shivering servant behind her, carrying her Prayer Book, dressed in
"a single lappet and without an handkerchief, &c. a well pointed satire
"on such persons as make themselves Singular with respect to Public
"Worship, merely to attract the notice of their neighbours, &c. &c."
Hogarth Moralized, page 154.

(g)   — Te sonantem plenius aureo,
Alcæe, plectro —— ——
Pugnas et exactos Tyrannos.   Horat: L. 2. Ode 13.

(h) A Latin Song called "Domum," sung with musical accompaniment, on the day before the commencement of their Whitsuntide Vacation, by the Scholars of Winchester College. The words "Matin Hymn, &c." in the preceding couplet refer to other ancient customs of that Venerable Seminary.

(i) The late LORD TALBOT, Steward of the Household.

> For an account of the MONASTERY of MEDENHAM, the Reader (if he thinks it worth his while) may confult the third volume of " CHRYSAL," or the Adventures of a Guinea.

(k) See Percy's Reliques of Antient Poetry.

(l) —— Hudibras gave him a twitch,
As quick as light'ning, in the br--ch,
Juft in the place where HONOUR's lodg'd,
As wife philofophers have judg'd,
Becaufe a kick in That Place more
Hurts Honour than deep wounds before.
>> Butler's Hudibras, Part 2. C. 3.

(m) The Old Pewter Platter, a pot-houfe in the neighbourhood of Hatton Garden.

(n) GOLGOTHA, " The place of a Scull," a name ludicroufly affixed to the Place in which the HEADS of Colleges affemble.

(o) Electrical fparks elicited by friction from a cat's back.

(p) The fociable Porker here alluded to, is well known to have been the affiduous companion of Lord M—t Edg——'s excurfions.

(q) On the death of Cibber the place of Poet Laureate was offered by Lord John Cavendifh, at the defire of the late Duke of Devonfhire then Lord Chamberlain, to Mr. GRAY, who refufed to accept it.
> See Mafon's Memoirs of the Life and Writings of GRAY.

(r) RUTTERKIN.—A Cat of this name was Cater-coufin to the great great great great great great great great great grandmother of GRIMALKIN; and Firft Cat in the Caterie of an old woman who was tried for bewitching the Daughter of the Countefs of Rutland in the beginning of the Sixteenth Century.

(s) " Moreover fhe confeffed that fhe took a Cat and chriftened it, &c. &c. and that " in the night following, the faid Cat was conveyed into the middeft of the

" fea by all thefe Witches fayling in their RIDDLE, or CIVES, and fo left
" the faid Cat right before the towne of Leith in Scotland. This doone,
" there did arife fuch a tempeft at Sea as a greater hath not been feen, &c."

" Againe it is confeffed that the faid chriftened CAT was the caufe of
" the Kinges Majeftie's fhippe, at his comming forthe of Denmarke, had
" a contrarie winde to the reft of the fhippes then b.eing in his companie,
" which thing was moft ftraunge and true, as the Kinges Majeftie acknow-
" ledgeth, for when the reft of the fhippes had a fair and good winde,
" then was the winde contrarie and altogether againft his Majeftie, &c."

Old Pamphlet entitled, " NEWES FROM SCOTLAND, &c. &c.
&c." Printed in the Year 1591, by William Wright.
See Notes on the Tragedy of Macbeth in Johnfon and
Steevens' edition of Shakfpeare.

(t) ———— Petit Ille dapes, ———— ————
Oraque vana movet, dentemque in dente fatigat:
Exercetque cibo delufum guttur inani,
Proque epulis tenues nequicquàm devorat auras.

Ovid. Met. Lib. 8.

THE END.

ERRATA.